LOYALTY

HENRY BRAUN

LOYALTY

New and Selected Poems

For Maggie Paul
fellow bard at
the Great Mother 2010

Henry Braun

Off the Grid Press, Weld, Maine

Published by:

Off the Grid Press
P. O. Box 84
Weld, Maine 04285

www.offthegridpress.net

Some of the poems in this book were first printed, or sung, in the following: *American Poetry Review*, *The Body Electric* (Norton 2000), *Poetry*, *The Maine Poets* (Down East Books 2003), *The Massachusetts Review*, *Painted Bride Quarterly*, *Continental Harmony 2000: A Hill in the Country*, *Franklin Journal*, *Lewiston Sun Journal*, *Maine Speaks* (Maine Writers and Publishers Alliance 1989), *www.poetsagainstwar.net*, *North Dakota Review*, *One Trick Pony*, *Off the Coast*, *The Cafe Review*, *The Blue Sofa Review*, *What Have You Lost?* (Greenwillow Books 1999), *The Vergil Woods* (New York: Atheneum 1968), *http://capa.conncoll.edu/braun.vergilwoods.html*, *Temple Road* (Nine Poem Press 2000).

Author photograph and cover art: *Terrain 1 (detail)*, by Joan Braun.
Book design by Michael Alpert.

Second Printing, 2008

ISBN: 0-9778429-0-8

CONTENTS

Dreamer 9

I.

Small Talk in Weld 13
Under Mt. Blue
   i. Growing Lettuce 14
   ii. To Bury a Bird 14
   iii. Ox 15
   iv. Reading Late 16
   v. Firewood Sermon 16
A Fellowship of Dowsers 17
Old Groups 19
St. Galileo 20
Getting over Habits 22
The Penlight 23
The Shed 24
A Poem about Everything 26
A Hill in the Country 27
The Great Rock in the Woods 28
Narrow Fellowship 29

II.

War Wheel 33
Shock and Awe 34
Angel of the War Years 36
Ushering in the Twentieth Century 37
The Poet-Priest 38

In Memory of Benjamin Linder 40
The Movement toward a New America
    in the 1960s 42
Bus Service in Buffalo, 1943 43
Crumbgiving 44
America in the 1930s 45
Growing Up in the 1940s 46
These Days 48
The Noise 49
The Book Spine 50

III.

Coming from Childhood 53
Stage Door Pop 54
Late Mail in Mt. Airy 55
The Sacred Same 57
A Boy Senses a Father 59
On the Road 60
A Certain Presence 61
An Excursion among Mountain Tools 62
Scholar Boy 63
The Professor 64
The College as Given 65
Blackboard Heaven 66
Writing Workshop 67
Hg, an Ode 68
From Porlock 69
Renga Rock 71
Kosher 72
The Little Cans 74
Why I Am Not a Scientist 76
Noah at Drydock 78
Thief of Permission 80
The Beginner 81
Dark and Light 82

IV.

Accessing Where We Are 85
Description of a Solstice 86
Another Solstice 90
A Limit to Naming 92
Concert 93
At the Met 94
An Ode to Fieldguides 95
So I Gather 96
Initiation into Chaos 97
In the Beginning Was the Middle 98
"Tradition" 99
Happy Dust 100
Loyalty 101

V.

From *The Vergil Woods*:
    Long Pull 105
    Adam Naming 106
    The Rape of Europa 107
    Sonnet in Winter 110
    The Vacation 111
    The Wrestlers 113
    My Crowns 114
    In Memory of My Father 116
    The Horn Waits 118
    Training the Eye 119
    My Road 120
    The Elements 121

Weight 123

for Joan, Jessie, Sarah, Natsuo, Sophia, and Elena,
and, of course, George

At night I go home to my country
in the waters of sleep
which is an island with a sea collar.
Each thing I own goes with me
to blossom Crusoe-like as island
fact and island figure, 2, 3 . . .
apparitional in moonlight. When
multitudes of memories crest a hill
I wait for their advent down, unafraid
even into my day.

The extra eyelid I wear
preserves my geography of dream.

I.

Blessèd small talk, now I understand
"Whew!" and "It's a wet one!"
  in the village store, in from the weather.
  All in the family, different families
  sound the surface of the skin
  worn so separately in common.
  The local watershed refills
  the wells of individual desire.

i. *Growing Lettuce*

I have broken soil
and run a line in the blackness with my finger
and dropped the flea-like seeds in
too thickly.

Even so, even so,
the lettuce comes, standing room only,
as a favor to a first try
and is a shy green.

ii. *To Bury a Bird*

Jump and ride spade
down for a deep one,
deep enough for the small.
Lever out the glossy
triangle, tearing grass hair.
In the far corner plant the bird,
a warble a grace note long
from the dark ages of bird song,
feathers, bones, and air.

iii. *Ox*

I marvel at the rope that holds me,
how it drops into its own thickness,

and the yoke too,
plant that rides me with hard thighs.

Landing on me now is the first snow,
the rain that takes time.

What season? I ask,
have to think,

have to begin to pull
on the syllables of winter.

For me, a field with a horse
is like a sentence with helpful punctuation.

iv. *Reading Late*

Some evenings fragility
lays itself out on roads
from the novel you are reading,
old peculiar enlargements
that keep you wakeful
long after the book closes.
Someone was alive
whom you followed by oil lamp
for hours through the pages
and now, in a quiet house,
everyone breathing must be looked at
and more than looked at,
accompanied.

v. *Firewood Sermon*

Sticks of wood are personalities
like dogs and cats, but simpler.
One hisses with the rain
garnered slowly on a woodpile. One
cackles cackles groans
and falls to its side.
Two, brought near, strike up an acquaintance
in the burning world.

With thirst
and no rods but their yellow
#2s, dowsers
are ranging toward the South,
ranging toward the North.
Attack scarecrows guard the farms.
Absentees sleep among the cobwebs.
One farm
to which a dowser comes,
magnetising the grains
that underlie the superhighways,
the muddy approach-roads of April,
is open and alone.

Across the valley,
barks adrift from a small dog.
Above the hills that *biforen us weren*,
clouds.
Grays of early evening cover the mosses
that cover the brook stones,
and Houghton's thread begins to lose its glint.
"On the one hand on the other hand" babble
its waters on their argument seaward.
A most clear of days—
each grain of dust was lowered by a raindrop
the stormy night before—almost is over.

Past the worn pungency of the outhouse
and past the shed's Servel
he climbs the hill.
His best eye catches a ghost going,
the part of himself that stayed behind as shepherd
for the eggs in twelves, the juice gallons,
the abundance of a young family
setting out its habits.
He stands in quiet near the cold cookstove
and later walks the land
of old wells dangerously lost
in second growth.

Elsewhere,
his brother and sister
dowsers are up in America,
and far,
far south the freighters move
patiently up and down between the oceans
that bathe Panama.
Houghton Brook adds its share.

We are the underground
of the tears of things
in rotogravure,
where Chekhov's brothers are watching
and a girl Robert Frost,
the other side of words.
Not a face is saying,
"I'm only a relative
of greatness in row two."
Each fills up a space
in separate life,
meals and the weather,
a try at coherence.
"Helping and serving"
is part-time, if at all.
Life is so heavy
in the old groups
that prophets are without honor.
What they have to go on
is love and a grudged OK,
the good that is always
coming out of Nazareth.

Someone is looking down
on lives from an airplane,
someone like me. I lift my eyes to the hills,
the small folds his shadow passes over,
to find him, hearing above
from all sides the OM of his engine
feeding on old sunlight.

In the metal bird someone like me
is homing in on the precious, the routine,
the daily round we move through in common.
In him as well the old
epistemologies keep trying
holds on the whole, the same
ten Thousand Things
wrestling the Weltanschauung;
parabolas lift from parabolas
to lengthen the experience of flying.

And I invoke
for such journeys the Christopher of motes
who knew the geometry of stigma,
the last Italian with a given name
alone, Galileo,
patron of free fall.

Whatever is above dwindles over
one man down in the quiet, fishing,

a meditation with a valence
of one,
or else building a fire
from memory with the two sticks of self
after and self before.

My nearest habit
is waiting in the kitchen
as a blind date with the food
I meet there,
and over I go to set
my hand to what my heart's
already set on.
Then a quick limb-fling down
to Heraclitus' brook
to see how the waters differ
from the last time.
           And back
up toward the white page, stopping
short for a chance
spillover from all the habits,
though usually not for long
enough. The next hump
is drawing me with its lode
and I journey on
to a quick read, a shmooz, or a sleep,
habit by habit across the hours'
delectable old hills.

When singing is a black sheep among sounds
in the wee hours, lightless you sing, you baaa
softly, reaching for the penlight,
feeling around for a scrap
to hold the rhythms of your dream
before the last mini-sleep,
before your gut is plucked
like a bass viol by the morning's
continuity.

An old silvery shed puzzles me with longing
and I free myself
by carefully slipping the reins from my shoulder
to follow.

But where? How can I move and keep the shed in view?
Easy metaphor
might close the road like a forbidding angel. I
need much more.

I need an art to live in henceforth as a life,
though I know it's true
that good insights radiate the day around them
joyfully.

One or two likenesses in tension together,
a piecemeal heaven,
a country shed gleaming for friends in the city
through my words,

maybe that's all I can have. And thanks for that too!
But some men have pulled
a heaven permanently down about our eyes
and staked it

like a great painfully beautiful circus tent.
Contemporaries
have taken that for the sky it is, our human
nature's sky.

So I start as usual on my home ground, a chair
and a long soft look
over the daily environment of known things
in fresh light

and address myself to the problem of the shed
and the gift of it,
not knowing if this is travel, sitting quite still,
or both at once.

A POEM ABOUT EVERYTHING, INCLUDING THE KITCHEN SINK

The little wings at Hermes' heels
are sufficient to provide the propulsion.
                                    –Bachelard

On our nubbled cellar wall
behind the machine sloshing the diapers
I pasted the Altamira bison.
Such good cutouts: soggy hillocks turning
over and over, plus the long gone
recalled to stick where it was,
now seeable again!

Everything in place, I flew upstairs,
feathers sprouting from my heels,
to follow Ms Fortune down the ink trail,
stuttering, stumbling sometimes,
to cellar music.

Everything relates
like the tips of my fingers fronting my chin
even as the word *so* widens in two directions,
so, so? (in Yiddish *nu*),
any tome whose spine
I lever from my shelves,
the dishes waiting in our kitchen sink
to randomly govern again *their* moment.

It isn't far in Maine
to the end of the past,
the quiet pipe, the random arrowhead.
The mountains are alone
with Thoreau's sun
in their ranges
and evergreens carpet all the peaks.

While on a moonlit night I fumble
to unlock the farmhouse,
the skyline of an old key
moves like a lost city.

On this hill whose curve
traces an indecipherable longing,
let me build my city,
the layer of all I saw and felt
a close cover on the naked rock
of Maine,
and in its hidden park
let me now closely learn
the mushrooms, the trees, the birds, the stars.

THE GREAT ROCK IN THE WOODS

for Matthew Gregor Goodman

It sees nothing where it has been seen
by all eyes in the climax forests
that pass in slow succession after fires.
Even the white bear may have known it
glazed by the last touch of the glacier
that, miles away, broke it off the mountain.
The story of its roll down here
to this surprising presence,
its ride with the field of stones
that made Maine hard to farm, and again hard,
is soon told.
          I take this boulder for a landmark
and pass by
in the deep woods on my road to friends.

Without a snake
I'd be obscurely hurt
as I gaze down at our sill
in the come-once-again summer.

There he is, glittering, dry,
an S on the too-near-to-mow crabgrass.

A memory of threat holds us
equally, though in Maine
zero at the bone is less mortal.
I'm proud to have him there sunning
after his slow
ascension,
his transport from a winter state of grace
between fat boulders in our cellar.

So be it!
Both of us awake
with jutting heads
at the startling starting line
of the present.

I I.

Certain crystals, the diatom, roll unseen in all we know. Gradually to the human plane came wheels, where the Aztecs sledged ashlars, the Esquimos over the land bridge traversed bundles, whole ages without the obvious, wheels came and meshed their teeth and turned and crushed by second nature, everywhere from hours square to desert sand wheels rolling forward around axles, the black holes of unrequited lov

We burn cities.
With your permission
the only animal that runs toward fire
to save, to gawk, to liven up the night,
cancels with fire the quick networks of borders.
I celebrate, with your permission, the borders
of human beings, the profiles lifting and turning
in drivers' seats, the parallels that bend
and meet at the tear ducts of the eye.
No longer frightened of fontanels,
I touch the soft craters of the mind cap
and root my nose gratefully in whorls
of babies' ears. I celebrate the skin,
the curves of women, the straight hips of men,
my hand with its own life
and tiny Pavlovian memories
of cusps in the arms of chairs and handkerchiefs
drawn like cold brooks through the fingers.
I sing the damaged hands of les Eyzies,
and Friday's footprint,
triangles in tempera of the holy.
As over the hump of windowsill more evening
crawls, I contemplate full moons
of countdown, after nine of which we come
with hanks of cord trailing from our bellies.
I celebrate, with your permission, the bellies,
the treasure kegs of aging males,
big bodies coming out of showers,

and the taut ramparts of little girls.
The approaching sine curve of an elbow
gazed at and touched by a pregnant woman,
I gaze at, and also touch, then sing
the double string between the eyes of lovers.
Faces, known and unknown, delineate
like the moon suddenly in breaks of cloud.
I celebrate and sing
all the beloved faces, all, MOAB,
and tickle the cittern for the cloud as well.
I wave as if positioned for goodbye
and, at the same time, for hello
in the borderless shadow of the lingam.

ANGEL OF THE WAR YEARS

for Father Dan, early 1970s

New angels were infolded among us
to share our daily bread and circus
and drink from our running cup.
Coming foreseen, one stood worn like a menhir,
grass pate flattened by the rain,
in a neighborhood two generations old.
Small children at the heart of meaning,
with the dew still heavy on our customs,
we were not ready for an angel,
but we took him in. And none of us asked for wings
or the tilt of flesh that breaks
common sunlight into halos.
His gestures were familiar: tired shepherd
after the parables begin straying
back towards the herd of what goes on.
With the quality of concern
one brings to a physician, we fed him
bread he praised and held in both his hands,
those famous days for the spirit,
deep within the intelligence of our houses
where the bookcases tower in the night,
seen from the outside dark by lamplight.

We have an affection for our tiredness,
now he is gone in the small German car,
for our peculiar brand of sadness.

Born like the rest of us as one,
there wasn't enough of him
for two women on a king-size bed,
a gravity for so much falling.

"Too many?" he asked with a frown
when he described his night to me.
Fifteen and shy with girls, I'd little
to answer this survivor of death camps.

He showed me blue numbers on his arm
as we watched again and again a screening
of *The Best Years of Our Lives*
at the Twentieth Century Theater
in Buffalo (owned by the Yellin family,
one of whom, Jack, had composed in the 30s
the Roosevelt campaign song
Happy Days Are Here Again.)

I can't remember my fellow usher's name.
He died young—in his king-size bed, I guess—
leaving an indissoluble legacy,
a seashell's, maybe, a softer one inside,
in the tide.

THE POET-PRIEST

for Brother Antoninus

Others were more at home with your long gown.
I understood the shoes that shined beneath it.
We sat above in tiers like angels
in the po-biz demonstration hall.

You kneeled in what we all
assumed was prayer, strode intently toward us

as if on a diving board, turned
and strode back. I felt accused,
caught there with stale expectation.

A teacher-priest with curls like Pan's
whispered "Well?" to his star
student, who answered "I'm not so sure."
"I'm not so sure, either."

You began to intone,
tying us to the blizzard outside,
a biblical connection
between tired birds and storms.
You squinted as if a vacuum
coveted your face.

Hefting your words we climbed the hills
and ran down, legs foreshortening, to a stop.
Then clapped.
The whole room stood and clapped.

You got down on your long
side below us like an auto mechanic
to readjust some more, if not to fix.

After a while with eyes
lifting slowly from the page,
one sees genera and kingdoms,
animal, vegetable, mineral.
Also, I
see the hair on my arm, fur
between kingdoms.
Twilight answers from its back.

I stand up in my room, yes,
to learn more than I know
from the news given away
by unfelt strokes of radar,
to hear
the voice of this
standing with bent head
under the stars.
On my wall the blue-
green cataracted eye, the planet poster,
hangs from its pin.

And so I ask again,
How much land, which land, does a man
need?
Wherever green is worn?
Or blue and white, red,
orange? Yes.

Yes,
when the little O,
this earth, wears the rainbow
raggedly, each man,
woman, child
needs
all.

After a while with eyes
returning slowly to the page—
yesterday's, today's—I say the names: Linder,
Schwerner, Goodman, Chaney, Corrie,
Ruzicka . . . Yes,
our land with all its names.

THE MOVEMENT TOWARD A NEW AMERICA
IN THE 1960S

in memory of Mitchell Goodman

Something large-scale was there
on the moving forward front. They
were the evangels
and carried the firecoal
from cave to cave
in the horn of an aurochs.

Pieces of the world fell, people
fell or, in famous cases, sailed
below the horizon.
There be memories
pulsing over the marsh-lit
terra incognita.

If more light's to be shed,
pen-thin rays will have to do
for starters, for *re*starters, in the dawn
of
of

Over the decades I raise my hand to speak
just so, as years ago I raised it
to clarify what standing alone meant,
a Jewish boy in short pants,
in the quiet of wartime America.

From the appearing point
there
between the gray buildings of Kenmore,

Come COLVIN-
CITY HALL! Burst forth,
old nodule of rocking-
growing light!
Become distinct as windows and a driver
and passengers going my way through the night.

CRUMBGIVING

for the Commander-in-Chief

Only from our point of view as masters of the table
does the eater of crumbs glow with a terrible
loveliness.
He clings to our pity like a bat,
certainly. And a few, independent of the prince,
think that disgusting, our table his rafter.
They miss the light in his eyes when we bowl him
the crumb.
For a moment he sees it with the fullest glance, a baby's,
his crumb beyond compare.
There is nothing else in his world but its hollows,
its rims,
bounding dreamily over the tablecloth like sagebrush.
From a distance he drinks the shadows in, facet by facet,
and swells.
What a pleasure to hear us, the masters, counting, two, ah,
three,
until, lovingly, it's his!

Remember us,
our chicken-in-every-pot,
our car-in-every-garage,
our Sears catalogue in every outhouse.

Moths hard on woolens
are beautifully, variably soft
on themselves.
              Have pity, moths!
We buried samples of our lives
in capsules at the fairs.
We watched King Kong
locked as chromosome on the Empire State,
watched the tiny extras, common men
in "men's hats," women in mid-length dresses,
scurry down city canyons in earthquake movies.

        In dream we imagined the Streamline.

Mornings of the Derby,
hours before the bluegrass shed its dew,
we placed our bets on Man of War,
on Whirlaway, on . . .

Please, Time,
           save,
save the proper nouns for our children!

i.

My first *Complete Shakespeare*, blue and heavy,
a birthday gift from my father,
lay on the table of our room.
I bent and riffled the onionskin for hours.
After his graveyard shift, my father,
dispatcher of the Aerocobra,
slept, a rising-falling, white-sheeted mound.
Our quiet was being fought for in Europe.
Japanese in khaki baseball caps
crouched on branches in the jungle.
We were in Buffalo, with great glacial lakes
above and below, and, to the side, Niagara.
Heavy with otherness, the young bookworm
omegaed from left to right across the page.

ii. *The Book of Knowledge*

Children who read before the war
knew all about the famous
7/8ths of the iceberg and
the Hindenburg held
swaying by the ring in its nose,
filled with mistaken H.

iii.

Aixo era y no era
(it was and it was not)—
so stories begin in Majorca.

My stepmother was a riveter, my father
a shop steward with sciatica.
On his high bicycle he pedaled
from grievance to grievance through the laboring nights.
I read, dreamed away in the outfield, and ate.
Cheese sandwiches (American on white)
take fingerprints when pinched,
and I pinched habitually at lunch.

During the war years,
when the game was always short of players,
everyone prayed and played.

These days the sunlight almost seems total.
A few men and women, trees, stand between heaven and earth.
In the light of their shadows we others are reading,
still,
messages the dead have stopped sending,
these days of almost fatal sunlight.

Now what has fallen where,
oh   my
world?

I am making limber a book spine,
backwards and forwards a stiff book spine,
in the only right way with a new one.
I knead and knead. After a while I bend down
to put my nose in the fresh smell of print,
then lean back to press more leaves from the middle.

Reaching the middle, I can read both ways,
backwards and forwards from nothing,
or stop before beginning again
a book with a limber spine useful for others,
stop at halfway what is not begun
except for the caress of dumb
and slow-working hands.

III.

When I come from childhood
with all my bridges alight behind
the stars are already named.

Pages of readouts
bulk in the observatories
with enough stars to shame Sumer.

I slow my breath to name
the burning bridges stars
still shining as my own.

Slow moving here
I am athletic in the dream world
whose cavern widens out from a man.
I meet him at the door
off a dark alley the artists use
on their solitary way to the footlights,
a grey-haired guardian in a sweater
whom everyone calls Pop.
Deep in his worn chair at the city's heart
he listens to the game on his radio,
springs up, and gathers in his arms
the roses for the virtuosi.
Over the years he'll tell
and tell again what only he saw plain
in glory at the old premières.
With Pop I reason all things out slowly
and then

      I leap,

           I leap from the wings.

Cars peel off from the Schuylkill.
How small the seamless triumph of peeling
off at 55 while talking quietly!
Yet, for another day, we all feel it.
Somewhere else
the mongoose and the cobra
hold each other's full attention.
It's time to stop paying mine
and come at last to down at the far end
of Wellesley Road.

Our little street
is getting on in years,
its oaks old enough now
to raise sidewalks on their own.
It's always a car coming
slowly through children
this way on summer afternoons.

The mailman's dog-awful hump of leather
lightens from door to door,
rousing once a day even the recluse
out of the deepest chair
through the lick of cobwebs.
And my letters glow,
an irregular pool in the sun
that still angles down from the mailslot.

The trafficperson's
red radish of a helicopter
thucks lazily above Mt. Airy.

for Hayden Carruth

In the present, higher on the same
fate wheel, nothing's wholly past.
The lion-women of memory
crouch in our cells, a plenitude of Gizehs.
Oceans with measured tides,
where the mollusks' soft ones/hard ones leave
indissoluble legacies,
push and pull us all.

And look!
        The foundation
stones of institutions,
those second-best answers to the grave,
keep being laid.

On *this* road one girl asks another,
"How *old* are you?"
              And we overhearers
slip into a mode of eternity.

Everywhere, the sacred same. It's everywhere.
Even democracies
break out a queen
for the harvest dance.

So how must *I* go
on the fate wheel?
Up and down, of course.

On course
on Pegasus.

A boy senses a father
baring like all men
his Achilles heel
lonely for the arrow
more slowly than anyone
who ages around them
but as surely.
Their love is a shore
every ninth wave of darkness
reaches. It is a ground
beyond words for a few words.
The biggest lie is speech
that breaks manfully out of silence
after its time.
Like this dervish poem
for the ear of the air.

Suddenly while driving,
heart furred with light
and charged for 70 years,
I connect the death of my father
with scraping the bottom of my car.

Huge   underground   is most
                    rock.

A small unyielding head rips a drive-train.

But
for the nth
time I overpass the fitting symbol
untouched
                    or lightly
touched.

Names of places decay.
Letters drop as if tongues were
a mountain range they tire of climbing.
Ranges of mountains, and the words
for whole countries soften
or harden, showing bone.
We try a new name for the inlet
where the huge rock holds its position
and the old tide turns.
Who we are is blurred.
Only our presence is certain
over the ground and water we keep
naming.

The Chouinard Chrome-Moly piton
and the Dolt Cobra—
who would not take them and go
on up to make a lovely killing
of himself on a rock face?
I, for one, so far, and most of my friends.

Would Belaying Gloves lengthen my adventure,
or the Cliff Hanger,
that "highly desirable tool
for the extreme artificial climb"?
I trust they would. They are so beautiful
in this catalogue, I want them already
to handle nicely and show on a flat table.

But I hear my old tools sighing, "Betrayer!
Have you forgotten your song
on the formal beauty of the crowbar
(ten pries from six directions!),
the peasant handiness of the pliers?
Stop whoring after strange gauds!"

I am pierced before I start my climb,
a figure of linguistic fun
who would pinprick the cliffs of fall
with his Grivel, his Crampus, his dream,
and his Stubai Nanga Parbat.

If you don't come I'm telling your Mommy

Asleep, his head on the *Britannica*,
aardvark to zzzzz, he knows
little of so much, little of the Great Plains
where "How" met "Howdy," or
the rattler's hidden nearness
and cool coiled attention (though
once he watched one at the zoo.)

He's learning the ultimate sticking points
partial to every individual,
the chakras and the Seven Deadly.
His Talmud is the public library
and *Everyman's*, $1 apiece, used.

A volume at a time, he's moving outward:
England, the Fertile Crescent, China . . .
Some night he'll share a moon
with half-seas-over Rihaku.

Always he awakens right at home.

I study the beam from the lighthouse
that plays its witness over
the in between and the peripheral.
Day by day I live its many lives;
by night, even when the sun shines, my own
over the same sea, close to the breathing,
my body more vulnerable than light.

A cold night and the hustle of horses
through the Appalachian woods
for hours gave us the college.
It seemed little more than a gatehouse,
though the log fire, the volume of Pascal
open on a walnut table,
made it college enough
in the early nineteenth century,
made the infinite silence less fearful.

The formulas appear, conserving themselves
back and forth over an equals sign—
any blackboard the address of heaven.
We call them down to earth,
hand them the apples of example,
our miles, our years.

                                Yet back and forth
in a pure grace like Gaston and Alphonse
sowing themselves before the doors of life,
they stay—

                God is one   but in hiding.
All men are mortal   but it feels unique.

There's no end
to the great creative innocence
that keeps sending, sending
the dear next ones
so openly among us.

For whole moments I find the years
unuseful.
Nothing comes to mind, nothing to tip
of tongue, not one stout Cortez of a word
to insert its human sound in the silence.

For whole moments, only
to be mortal and have successors
canted around this table like an edge,
each one toward his darkness, her sunlight.
And . . .

Ductile is the rope that draws
the young centaurs.

Dropped in the middle of the haves
and the have nots are we,
Hermes' poets, honorary haves, drops
of mercury (let's say)
hunching our shiny backs inward,
unlured (mostly) by their ribbons.

Not an oil and not a water
but an *element*,
citizens of our own liquidity
offended at being seen as silver
going for the gold, we're mercurial
makers of verses . . .

Suppose they tap us,
what do they see?
Neither kegs, reservoirs, nor faucets,
just *us* snugging back to poems,
which are ourselves,
like the children of old families,
loyal, dear Hg, to a fault.

My simulacrum
at the kitchen table of the doll's house
crosses his tiny legs,
stretches the leather of his tiny slippers
by flexing and unflexing his big toe,
and writes

In Xanadu did Kubla Khan
over again.

He too comes from a dream,
being, in his own way, the man from Porlock
on the road over a hundred years, and well read.

Now he rests and works
hidden in the countryside of culture
measureless to man
these days and, for that matter, to the Mongols.

Over again he calls up damsel,
Abyssinian maid,
and is himself aroused to the vision . . .

Could I revive within me . . .

Without interruption he grows to human height
along with the whole doll's house, now a lonely
farm house:

Since there is room for
poem after poem about this earth,
a few might as well be his.

A bird first, then a snake, then a toad,
my evening walk.
Whatever comes next, friendly to creation.

A slammed cardoor alerts the wilderness.
A slow raising of heads.
The moon watched by Leopardi governs.

An axle settles in a budding grove.
Somewhere in the anthill is just right.
The 19th century's leaning against trees is over.

Oil flowers on the pools.
The zoo's bear   differs.
The bear   at   the zoo.

A bottle in Maine.

Virgin Maine.

The woods now are all garden.
Not even sandgrains are clones, nor snowflakes.
We travel to the moon in silver clothes.

The car, after mountainclimbing seen, how foursquare!
Ant-meets-wall-its-six-feet-never-miss-a-step.
The rubythroated Clytemnestra.

Something knows the temperatures of water,
iron, and the thingless air. Something
inside us remembers
the last mass of drops in every cup
and the number of bell peals.
To the desired hour it comes and awakens.
We move
into action good and bad, to virtue, sin,
just as in the old days.
Something knows   though living blurs it over.
We eat what's advertised in our direction
and half forget
which tree was kosher, which treyf, in the Garden.
                    (Who walks here now? With whom?)
Among us outside, the serpent's
progeny slither on the ground to counsel.

Tonight from the Buffalo of my childhood
one street, TACOMA, appears.

                                        Why
always does it feel
there's something ultimate to say
for one or two streets in a city,
words to balance what the painters show,
the Masaccios, the Hoppers,
some clarity about the lost
becoming in itself a liberation?

I see like a Jewish Edward Hopper
         (by inward eye if not with outward hand)
Simon's Confectionery, the butcher
Sultanik's

בשר כשר

on the plate glass

lit from within
under a solitary streetlamp.

Observers alone with all we know,
it is our watch   just for having been born.

Father forgive
what a chip off the old
block is doing.
I'm leaving your turrets behind
for a glean in the vulnerable
field where the soybeans are and the loose figs.
I'm leaving your Carcassonne
of canned goods, of food
according to Euclid:
the diced carrots and the baby limas
in cylinders of silver;
the Pet Milk and the large Carnation;
the world of tiers of rims
congruent, Campbell's rampant;
the *aes triplex* of Spam
(whose key I learned to turn without bloodshed);
the first Shredded Wheat, Niagara Falls *bouffant*
(a whole childhood's worth of contemplation);
hash with its rubbery flabs
drownable in ketchup's sole variety;
the portly rooks of juice on the high shelf;
all the little meats salted with tears,
olive loaf, Thuringer, baloney,
for the white bread America had come to.

Father, whom the Depression drove
behind those silver ramparts,
I have inherited the armoire.

I am as sanguine for the little cans
as you were.
But, *lech lecha*, I go,
knowing what I do,
from behind the ramparts to eat
the praiseworthy food of the hippies,
risking decay, weather, and the harvest.

Sundays in the quiet science building.
My hotelière
of the elemental,
my friend in white,
lays the table before me
so, the 100 proof
proof: the ball on its inclin-
ing plane, the water spark-
broken into gasses.
She demonstrates the world that is
and is not mine,
for whom the elements
are not, as by latest count, 106
but earth, air, fire, and water,
the old contenders for
my naked eye.
If like an Ionian I had to
pick one, one thing everything is made from,
I'd be dumb. Earth?
Air? Fire? Water?
Some of each, thank you, is what I'm after,
have been all my years. At 70
it's far too late
to nominate
a substrate.
Chaos more or less benignly reigns
for me and mine,
chaos and old day.

As for this killing field
and resurrection ground
of the minute
minute particular, the act just so,
just and so,
endlessly reenacted—
I am allowed to come
and watch
her desire to share
burn condescension to a fine ash.
For I too was born in Scientia
and naturally desire to know
this way as well.

On Christmas day when I was 12
near midnight, I aligned the labels
of tiny wooden barrels of sulfur,
calcium carbonate, and charcoal,
and sat in quiet proud attention,
a novice in prayer
before the triptych of my Gilbert
#10 Chemistry Set.
My father slept. The Bunsen burner was awake.
It felt like Sunday
in a quiet science building.

Never having been just here before
just now, I'm slowly scanning the rains
as I sit, my lap the pole-star for
Glasnost, one aging cat, and Tyrone,
the other. A hate affair, theirs, lifetimes long.

A crow's footings on my face, La
Fontaine's forky mapguide
toward self as *alter kocher*; fear,
with magnetic precision,
alighting as tabby on my heart's
most accessible of ledges;
with crystalline
clarity tiny
erosions within
downloading signals from the Big One . . .

9 gathers and 5 releases
in the land of the am and the pm
away from where I scribble.
What *is* time, this clocktime,
its hands always on its face,
moving relentless peek-a-boos along?
Can I express its . . . *sunyata,*
the emptiness
that mirrors the dustmotes landing,
Glasnost and Tyrone passing?

If you want a bold assertion,
behold a mountain against a sky.

I'll go there
for my while
as the dot end
of a meiosis!

Ararat, ahoy!

A thief lives on the side where my eyes were.
I glance back and forth
with my day vision and my night vision. And eat carrots.
But he gets around me.

Were my head all eye, a ball that tells all
the present to itself—then,
ah then I would find this thief,
deny him what he takes,
my sense of permission to live freely
and make freely.
                       But my eyes are
slow slits that close half the time
to rest their blindness for the other half.

Sometimes, though, all a-prong I act
as if the thief permitted,
going very far out, laughing, giddy, serious,
until the permit's stealthily withdrawn.

He trusts himself to the finest of mirrors only,
oval pools wreathed in wooden armor,
and walks between his chosen glows.

Surprise him with individuals slowly,
this young knight bent within the family moat.
The blocknote, say, of a random woodpecker,
a fir framed a mile from the castle
in those languidly lifted oculars,
or the most swelling cumulus ever
smack above his forest.

O there it is,
a not-me, a not-me, and another
not-me, each thing gathered as one
after one complete in our common world.

Let him come now. I think he's ready
for unimagined joy
in our unprepossessing wilderness.

Suddenly it is not sudden,
my standing beset
among the generation with made faces
on my own built hill
from which the words reach further
and fall down from higher.

On similar piles my peers,
greying faster than they meant to grey,
startle like me.
It happened while we watched it
not really happening
in the dark and light of the sun.

Young one day and not so young
the next and then young
once more—that was the way
and is. Maybe for a long time,
though time on the new plateau
one life wide
across from the others.

IV.

We come from the country of the typewriter
with an ancient clacking accent. The platforms where
our fingers made speeches letter by letter
move not. Or move only a bit, not byte.
Death is the leveller of tools
too. The dream
of every man a Gutenberg in little
fades into cyberdawn.

My Corona
intimately lives with rain, its "I"
stayed in a rusted gesture of goodbye.
My Hermes, my Remington,
all the old streamlines,
meet in infinity of nothing's
fridges and tail-finned cars.

It is enough, *daiyenu*, it's enough
being here in the sitting position,
me and my
Toshiba with its bundled windows
alone in the early sun.

DESCRIPTION OF A SOLSTICE

for Natsuo

i.

Through quiet midnight
the past dovetails with the future
and we have a city
in full day.
And still
in Philadelphia
the heaven of the blueprint governs
the mortar's slap,
the lodgment of the brick,
mute arcs swinging on a crane.

We come as family
in twos and threes, molecules of love.
We rise up
in the old neighborhoods
where giving in a sandgrain at a time
equally governs.

Our hills shoulder more than Atlas.

In libraries, college sheds,
the gables of la bohême,
the unmoored
accumulate like clouds, big lost cerebra.
The mulling over from odd angles
begins.

Or sunbathing
with closed eyes down a silver funnel.

In the Northern Liberties
the church with a gold dome welcomes sunlight.
At 30th Street
under the high clerestory of the station
people like to stand
and see others with gold flecks around them.

Veni Creator Spiritus!

ii.

Whatever happened
to laying on of hands
and the gift of tongues,
the world folded in the altarpiece?

I know,
what was all
is now some
and lives in a museum
supplemented by a café-bookstore.
In art
it's OK to approach the king.

I work at my fit each morning,
this comfort to the age's terror.
I am a child of God.

Serious secular
waiting equals prayer,
and is my work.

I know,
hearing the birdcall,
I'll see the bird too
if I wait right,
if I wait.

iii.

It is so quiet I hear
the silk dress of my own breathing,
and I desire myself
as I am best, a leaner forward
with widened eyes, a listener.
Though I arrest myself
years later
for having left the scene
of opportunity,
I know the scene is always me
in a little plenum of a world.

Often I find when looking back
the count is higher than I thought.
So subtractable 1930!
I was complete in July, a 9 lb. Vishnu
floating inside a young Irishwoman.
My new name waited on her lips.

By and large, I was born

        and am reborn

        in complementary rings

        around some hidden core

which probes all levels like a solstice:

a lint-fringed paramecium

flirting with him and her

self *sub oculo,*

filings huddling in magnetic fields.

        Adam and Eve, the forked pair,

        ignite my memory like flints:

        an' sh' wore a nekkid dre-ess

        for slow kissing's fishnibbles,

        the laying on of hands, the gift of tongues.

        iv.

        Soft familiar summer shoe,

        your laces leap

through the bent justice of the eyeholes,

        tick and tick and tick.

            The motions of

        swimming

            disenhibernate.

I'll walk upon the beach, if not

with a young man's pharaonic stride,

at least with even shoulders and clear eyes.

i.

Years go by and then you know
the quarks of love
are transience and desire,
a hand grabbing a sweet
while leaving childhood,
a man and a woman
three-scoring in a mirror, a little
lower than the angels!

ii.

All in view
like the sun going down
we begin winter
with a bow.
Spruce and fir
tall in the dooryard
give themselves over
storylessly.
Spring's
days of glory be
are waiting behind the wind. It's
time to go back in.

iii.

Home is where you find things
flawlessly in the dark, shelves
of now-to-be-always half-read books,
classics cut out from heaven
with timeless scissors, windows
and skies behind the way glass stops the fingers,
Bach's music and its mother
silence.

iv.

In my song as
in goat song
the burden turns
as the ox plows.

The pleasures of a first protractor
awaken the Giotto in a boy, and the Euclid,
perfect circles, the mouths of angles
opening and closing,
the hypotenuse sure of arrival point to point.

Grown, he learns
the patience of parallel lines
that meet, as they say, in infinity.
He lives by naming left right up and down
the unblurred shapes of things,
a popple leaf pivoting in the wind,
the tail of an imaginary mermaid.

No longer early when it comes,
the setback of setbacks to the very ground
of non-being in tunneled soil,
has already its ancient names,
thanatos, pallida mors, forgotten
syllables moaning in Neanderthal.

No Giotto, no Euclid, perfectly encircles
that—in any language with a name.

The woman who crouches lovingly
against the wingbone of her harp,
the leglocked cellos
gyroscoping on their pivots
in the fluttery happiness of fame,
the sounds themselves, all, all
body forth their parts
when the conductor's hands
leapfrog toward one Pythagorean length.

Blessed art!
As in a Giotto
a room's forms
are made to listen to gold's
deepest dialogue with light, so
here. Here is the room of restoration
for those who walk away from lost causes
clenching empty hands in their pockets,
for those contorted by a daily round.

As long
as movements sound
their good speed.

What sound's to be made before a painting?

Ruisdael and Hobbema,
the road commissioners of Haarlem,
with spat and brush for giant rake and shovel,
show here,
ornately rectangled
in wood, here in upper Manahatta.

More alien than hermit crabs
in a forest?
Yes, so lucidly
so.

Hear,
o museumgoers, art and the world
is one
hand clapping.

Glossy *Peterson*, erotic like the world
herself with corvids and raptors and warbler variations,
all winter I gaze over your pages.
                                        And you fish,
shown in full profile tail to nose,
minnowed horizontally at separate levels,
each with a startled eye.

Trees!
A fashion show of towers
of Being needled, leaved, and flowered.

And rocks too.
May I address your gneiss,
your mica's handy chunks,
as bards address the mother they're torn from?

Ah my Guides, you seem the very placenta
of Venus, conurbations in winter
trawled over at midnight by a traveler's eye
from the page-sized window of a stratoliner,

a plenum of . . . plena, motionlessly real
with birds, fish, trees, rocks, and more

'Summer afternoon,' the most beautiful
words in the language.

–Henry James

All thumbs, none green,
I gather for the gardenless
wildflowers come upon singly.

Here's the clammy albino
mushroom posing like a bluebell
newborn from hell,
Old Man's Beard close by Virgin's Bower,
and down our unmowed path
one lotus rafting on its pond.
Then, more than the itself of the bug,
a waterwalker's shadow lengthening its sprawl
as just another.

So on my summer afternoon I gather
my chances, each distinct among
the contradancing double helices.

My first pronunciation of "chaos"
created laughter.
I was twelve
and doing *Genesis* in Hebrew school.
"Kows?" "Kaa-ohs?" How could I know?
How *could* I know?
And trilobite with the reversed *l b*,
Plato with a flat *a*, Aristotle accented
on the second syllable—
tribolite, Pl*a*to, Ar*i*stotle. . . .
A quiet boy, I read before I said.

Gradually it all came out kosher,
as it were, "trippingly on the tongue."
I emigrated from my social class,
another raznochinets
whose true country is a bookcase.
Now,
                          ah now,
I live in faith with "the meaning-
bearing nature of system violations,"
the strange attractors of my only life.

Nothing really begins
save to emphasize
an already wholly given
elsewhen.
Even amoebas
wriggled in the pre-bloodstream of a middle
eon. Bundles of reeds from the Nile
became the columnar
emphases of the Doric.

Begin with noticing the middle,
the Przwalsky horse, say,
a quiet stubby grazer
inheriting, initiating
bloodlines.

Begin with everyday.

The wheels we travel on roll inwardly,
tightening to scrolls
for the Memorial Library
of travel.

"TRADITION!"

Tevye the dairyman

In my bluest notebook
pointed to by the dog ears
are phrases I am always thinking
as my dearest own,
flesh of flesh and bone of bone.
They are, nonetheless, all quotations
naked without marks,
mitochondria from the mother lode.

And so I live to quote,
quote, quote what's already
outside in the world
as common as the unseen
air.

This happy dust   the body
rises
Magdalenian still
crouched   and with its rush-torch
uplifted
enters the next room
of its aging.

LOYALTY

Each morning the shining
ball lifts over the ridge
to warm my Subaru
where I dwell, where I live it up,
in the between while
learning how
not to hurt the way
falling leaves surround
a wholeness of life,
not to see
fringes of the ocean
other than fresh and old,
not to sift the grains
of wheat and sand we are given
and given
overly carelessly.
                 My smile
is too much backed by consciousness
for me ever to die.

So much for gravity!
hums the hummingbird
eyeing my eye.
It's time
to adjust my hover-buckle
to the task,
faithfully to repair
our Hubble
with all the other bees at work
on the starflower.

V.

I am here
rowing backward from my poems
and the poems of others.
Goodbye. How could I stay
at the dock of their homecoming?
I row from summer
with its flickers and cold stoves
on the long pull.

Behind me the abyss
thunders around its parched
coinspace of an eye.
Perhaps the coin is stamped
with a first noun.

I will row home
when the shore is strange enough.

ADAM NAMING

My body is tired for the birds that have flown from me;
Their fathomless wings are riding from my brow
In echoes. I have finished naming now:
They are not lost that fall by an unmapped sea.

Twilight is home for wrens in the great oak trees
And for the hawk that in grey caves has lain,
The peacock, host of the rainbow after rain,
And river swan, pearl of earth's necklaces.

Nests are arrayed and shingled in the air
Beneath the wandering aegis of a word
Chosen by me. When mating calls are heard
My poem moves in the desiring pair.

Envied by huntsmen I numbered the animals
Gathered from nature in my baptistery;
The unicorn pranced, eyes arched in mystery,
And zebras passed musing on parallels.

I have uplifted tents within my mind
For timeless griffins with vague wings outspread
And serpents of the field. Even the dead
Are sung and not to quietness resigned.

They have all gone like music from my keeping
Towards the named world. Left in this silent garden,
Tired of my duties as its lonely warden,
I seek forgetfulness at last in sleeping.

after the painting by Titian in the Gardner Museum, Boston

He offered himself as game for women's hands
If they could lay to bulls that kind of straying
Idly beyond the reasonable fence and the square bull pasture
Towards the river side. He stopped their playing,
Made them fall back astonished by the sand
As, unforeseen, his gentleness alarmed.
Then, in fear of heightening their fear,
He paused and wonder danced alone in the air between.
His lung was quickened presently by a girl
Bolder than all the rest, sidling with laughter towards him.
But for the river she was all that moved,
A plait of flowers in her hand, desire in her limbs
For motion in the pattern of a dance
And the heaviness of strange intent about her.
Is there a heart not gathered by faint swaying,
This way, this way, accompanied by laughter?
Far within the circles of his body awakening
And moving at first outwards came the bull.
He tapped once, bowed his head and tapped again
As if to shake off springs of violence,
Then sank, for his great body was allayed
Partly and without malice he gazed there.
Soon the cowering girls made a ring about him;
Europa set her wreath upon his horns.
A silence fell that gave voice to the river
And the chapped rush of leaves. Then with a sigh,
As the Europa in each girl was loosed
To a corporeal rhythm, dance began.

Figures insinuated by desire
Flashed forth, evoking mushroom agonies
Or little wildernesses of turmoil
In the surprised beholder. Yet the dance
Trimmed their incipient fire to pattern still.
And the quiet music was answered by the bull
Only with breathing and abstracted eyes.
They were displeased by so much darkness garnered
Slothfully there and longed to see it rise.
Some struck him as they passed with whips of scarves
And some threw flowers. At last Europa dropped
Upon his back and stroked the glacial hide,
With her moist hands exploring pallid folds.
He could not bear the weight of that last garland
And all the impositions on his mood
By careless girls. He roused himself, therefore,
Out of the invisible chains of simple being
And joined them, moving faster as they moved
Until his foot was light with that sweet dancing.
But they are often slain who play with darkness
Or left behind near the original ground
Raising bruised fingers toward a blind ascension.
The bull, aflame, sprang for the water. Cries
Rebounded as if laughter struck blank walls
And the disheartened ring of virgins, flower
By its own beauty spoiled, fell back and broke.
Then they came together, as we see them here,
Trailing along the distant water's edge
Like the shucked petals of a ripened tale.
Clutching a horn, as her part taurine gown
Already mingles, chosen Europa rides.

The bull has leaped at once through sky and water
To harmonize with that which most dissolves;
He pulses toward fulfillment on a groundswell,
Followed by what the stewpots of the sea
Exhale: a fish flecked with the primal sunlight,
Runnels of foam. Love's bedfellows are here,
Planing the unforgettable blue in chubby disarray,
Their arrows bathed in Alpine clarity.
It is the seed-time of myth, strewing and passing over;
As in an hourglass when the sand drops free
The future spreads inexorably. Onward,
Where shafts of rock hoist the aspiring wave,
A couch is set; within an open meadow
A tentative cradle waxes in its tree.

Now stretch pale fibers of the day again
And the vast weaving that the sun betrays
Is lying open to the winter rain.
All color is an echoing of greys
Half danced to by the jagged evergreens.
The field's impassioned flowers have fought the sting
Of the cold long ago. A mandrake leans
In a locked swamp, the ice's overhang.
Shadows toward night grow till they loop the world.
The curved blade of their East cuts one by one
Dark patterns on the landscape. Soon the cold
Of light will tunnel through the air alone
And men will know how little can satisfy,
Watching a lonely star possess the sky.

No one to referee that game,
Poor fledglings, with their heads thrown back
And mastered hips joined to their shame,
Are lonely partners on the rack.

Who is that watchman of the night,
Stretched out, staring so vacantly
From his filled bed until the light
Of day permit activity?

And who lies breathing at his side,
In sleep a kind of ruffed grouse?
Is it the girl that neatly glides
About the duties of her house?

They married decent strangers; she
For images of his despair
Without her, for his good name; he
For guilt and the curling of her hair.

Yearly to interpose delight
They go upon their honeymoon
Again, where things are never quite
The same although they should be soon.

And a small cottage has sprung up
Near a favorite swimming cove;
Every summer they come up
To localize their straying love.

On starry nights after their meal
Old rituals of hand in hand
Begin and what they think they feel
Makes them lie upon cool sand.

So they tumble by that shore
Of the uncaring upland lake
As if it were not done before
And each moans for the other's sake.

Yesterday, after twenty years,
Schools, businesses, and wars,
I met my wrestling partner Bert
B. He was the boy who taught
The nelson, half and full, to the grammar school.
But Bert was no fool;
He kept tricks in his bag. I tried,
And when "Uncle" was cried for, I cried,
Holding out longer if girls were there.
He is a bull now. I am a bear;
Neither wants to talk for long—
But, yesterday, in a glance it seemed
Our little lost bodies sprang
Toward sweat and the mat again.

MY CROWNS

for Dr. Pontifex

That was wings too,
like everything not rigid,
everything between two
people or a people and its city
or a cloud and its sky.

The dentist and I
worked my teeth for half a year,
the New Boston rising from its pad
outside our window.
And as he drilled deeper
the development reached higher
and I grew older
until all was capped with gold:
his fee, the sky,
the stumps that lined my jaw,
that aching row.

I am complete now
though the city is still changing.
I miss the man
whose intelligence
lay wholly in his competence,
all clouded beside.
Such friendships end
when the skill that called them up has run
its course.

Everything human has wings
(better to name it that than decay)
and flies toward an inevitable future:
a city, a body, warmth between two men;
everything has its day—except,
of course, my golden crowns.

IN MEMORY OF MY FATHER

i. *The Newspaper*

A strange seduction.
I find myself a young man
in my father's habit,
his old browsing eternity
with the news.

All of it feeds me—
the sports and the comics,
the front page with its many graves,
editorials,
horse-blinders and loss.

When we were in this life together
I read like an educated man.

ii. *Where it clearly stops*

Almost a child again, grown from wading,
I walk past the end of your life
where it clearly stops.

iii. *The Steel Ball*

The best of what they say means
"You've got the steel ball
  that we had."
  Hardly a word more that's right,
  as if to describe
  something so round
  and so around
  were impossible.

I've got the aching steel ball.
Oh I've got it
to come on or be come on by
each day while it grows small.
Keeping faith,
I approach the ball as a kind of life
whose feeling I now hold
in trust, waiting somehow.

Where is eternity? I am looking.

In a room I was getting used to
I found in dust beneath the couch
a microscopic hunting horn
I lost as a child.
(It is my luck to find the things I need
exiled from where I lost them.)
Dust, gentle dust,
coated from my eyes the horn rungs
and stopped, an ageing hill, the mouth of the horn.

I reached down, but my fingers would not take it
as they sloped like pagodas over it.
My eyes began to blur.
And now the couch is back, corner on corner.

Inviolable dust,
there seemed, as always in your little worlds,
a chance to set out again through deserts.

TRAINING THE EYE

for Oscar Sanborn of Weld

It seems the corridors of my childhood
live behind me and shrink as living people:
the one at grammar school I stumbled down
alone during classhour, sick to my stomach,
it was a kind of endless Karnak
as I wound my arms around a pillar
and said, "I will remember this forever,"
noting within my nausea.

It's there, unfairly small,
as our assembly hall is there
with its picture, "The British Burning Buffalo."
Each of the colors is an orphan
now that I've grown, seen Turner and Renoir.

But can all this be so
in the gradual world of villages?
Few leave to be surprised at a dog's growth
on their return, or a field of trees—
the sadness of losing out from watching.
And death diminishes like the road from town.

MY ROAD

Because there is always craft
I have not looked you in the face.

What am I to do with
what I cannot understand,
the ground and the brook and the tears in my eyes?
Not to have been born
is the best friend
of the pure particular places.

My hand's as good as any toad;
the different flashes of my clothes
go with the grass—
something to touch is not the bigot.
What am I to do with
what I distill,
an anger in the breathing?
How can I narrow further to the saying?

When I'm working I see the grass most clearly,
the orange alder root at home
in tough bourgeois
possession of the soil,
and, after nights of rain,
gentle mud laminating the ditches.

The elements I have by heart
are stone and water.
Happy the poets with all four!

I buy and grow
and sleep with my collection,
take inventory too:

And then, for any day,
a bug climbing a brick is,
with the right hold of my mind,
Sinon climbing the walls of Troy
or the hero, on all fours, over
the pit in Haggard's *She*.

I am afraid to see my life this way,
though every year
like Actaeon I mislay the fear
at times out of time
that strangely devour and leave one.

The bug goes on with his instinct
over the brick the seasons wear,
with hours enough to get a life in.

We are given weight
separate from the earth
as the first miracle,

a certain leave
to rise like the stones
in a thawing road.

There are directions
pointed to by growing
in the flowering branch

or the equal root for those
who have tried and tired,
who disbelieve the sunlight.

Because it is lonely,
teachers wait at the mouths of caves
for our coming home.

Henry Braun was born in Olean, New York in 1930 and grew up in Buffalo. After graduating from Brandeis University, where he studied with Claude Vigée and J. V. Cunningham, he spent a year in France on a Fulbright Scholarship, and then went to Boston University, where he participated in Robert Lowell's workshop. In the 1960s he organized poetry read-ins against the war in Vietnam and was convicted in a Federal court of tax evasion. His war tax dollars were donated to a veterans hospital and to public schools in Philadelphia. As an organizer of a draft card turn-in at the Justice Department, he was an unindicted co-conspirator at the "Boston Five" trial.

Most of his career as a teacher of literature and creative writing was at Temple University, including a year at Temple's branch campus in Japan. He has served as coordinator and host of the Poetry Center of the YM-YWHA in Philadelphia. In 1968 his first book of poems, *The Vergil Woods*, was published by Atheneum. His work has appeared in many magazines, including *Poetry, The Nation, The Massachusetts Review, American Poetry Review, Prairie Schooner,* and *The Colorado Review,* and in several anthologies. He now lives with his wife, the artist and family therapist Joan Braun, off the grid in Weld, Maine.